ANGEL
CITY

For Leon Graves and Roy Chung.

For Patti Gauch, who believed.

For Al Mantini, un buen hombre.

For my Georgia friends, Jean Bell Willhite and Suzanne Howlett.

For Carole Byard, who gave her heart to this book.

—T.J.

To Michael and Millicent, my faithful guardian angels,

Michelle, my loving cousin,

and my niece, Michelle.

Thank you, Mr. Ricky.

—C.B.

ANGEL CITY

WITHDRAWN

3 1901 04400 9597

Tony Johnston   *illustrated by*   Carole Byard

PHILOMEL BOOKS

Dawn grays Los Angeles like a great pigeon wing.
Old man Joseph plods along, alone.
Past the homeless sleeping
like small lost boats,
past buildings that tilt
their old chins toward the sun,
past a wall pocked
with bullet holes.
He hears a sound
coming from a Dumpster—a whimper frail
as life.

It is a baby, perfect and new. Swaddled
in dawn.
Old man Joseph grunts. "Angel City. Humph.
Where's the angels? Where's the love?"
Bundling it in his jacket, close to him,
he takes the baby home.

The baby's squall is shrill.
It fills old man Joseph's small room.
The child makes sucking sounds,
its tiny lips seeking milk.
Like a large strange bird,
the old man clucks to it.
"Ain't no bottles here," he says, "but beer."
His neighbor Mrs. Perez has got proper bottles.
And milk.
She shows him how to warm it,
to test it on his wrist.
"He is my gift from God," says the old man.
"I aim to care for him."

He names the baby Juan.
All day, he hovers over him,
humming "Georgia on My Mind."
Georgia's where he's from.

The old man has promised to raise that baby.
Damned if he won't.
Slowly, he learns old mysteries—
of diapering and burping and spitting up,
the feel of a baby full of sleep.
When *he* goes sleepless, he looks skyward
and grumbles, "Promise still holds."

Juan is a Mexican baby. He needs to know
Mexican things.
So old man Joseph consults his neighbors
about *those* mysteries.
Mrs. Gonzalez presents him with a recipe
for *chiles en nogada*—"*para* when Juan's *grande.*"
Mrs. Perez gives him instruction in tamales.
In the kitchen, while little Juan sleeps,
they fill corn *masa* with fragrant meat.
While she cooks, Mrs. Perez chirps a song
about singing flowers.
The old man fumbles with the tamales
and with the song. *"Ay-ay-ay-ay! Cant-on los flor-ies!"*
He intends to learn Spanish
for that tiny baby.

The days go quickly, gulped down
like milk.
Now Juan is one.
He is learning to walk
on his plump legs. He stumbles a lot.
Mrs. Perez has taught her neighbor
a get-well chant:
Sana, sana, colita de rana,
Si no sanas hoy, sanarás mañana.
The old man chants that a lot.
Seems to help small hurts. But every day
he worries about other wounds.
From knives. From guns.
There's a tree outside, hunched over
from bucking the wind.
Every day he sees that tree and thinks,
I do my best, but I can't keep Juan
from the wind.
"Lord," he prays, "maybe you can."

Soon Juan is two.
Old man Joseph sees that he learns
Georgia things.
Georgia tunes, Georgia vittles, Georgia flutter fans.
Summers, when heat smothers Angel City,
he whittles fans for them.
Fans like large insect wings.
They sit outside and flurr the air. Two big bugs.
Sometimes he hugs Juan
for no known reason.
Sometimes Juan does the same.
The old man loves the tales of Africa
that his grandpapa told to him.
Often, through thin walls, Mrs. Perez hears
"In the beginning—"
His voice sings like a fine-skinned drum.

Old man Joseph's handy. Sees to most needs
in his apartment building. Like plumbing.
While the old man fits pipes and snakes out drains,
Juan swashes toilets with a long-armed brush,
for fun.
Creates small indoor rains.

In the barrio old man Joseph hears of a mural,
a vast wall splashed with the angry paint
of the great David Siqueiros.
When they go there, he leans close
so Juan, piggyback, can get a good look.
"Though he's only three," he tells everyone,
"my Juan needs to know great art."

Old man Joseph loves popcorn.
Whenever he can scrape up a little stash of cash,
he splurges on some.
He heats it in a saucepan with a lid. Shakes it a lot.
When the kernels start to hop,
he mutters, "Pop-pop. Pop-pop."
Juan calls him "Pop-pop."

Juan is already four and sprouting up
like a flower.
Time to time, Pop-pop scours the trash for cans
to turn in, to buy little extras for his son.
When he scrimps together enough,
he gives Juan a box of crayons.
Juan squeals with delight,
then snaps them in two, like beans.
While the old man heats SpaghettiOs,
Juan crayons on the wall.
Pop-pop sighs. "Perhaps that's how Siqueiros began."

One day Juan is five. Ready for school.
Because he's so anxious about that,
Pop-pop packs Juan's lunch
the night before—a tamale and sugared grits.
He remembers the night he found Juan.
Remembers the bullet-wall's scarred face.
He still hears spurts of gunfire,
sometimes, in the barrio. And his heart hurts.
"Angels done flown
this coop," he whispers. "Where's the love?"
So every day he walks Juan to school,
and walks him home.
Sometimes people watch them and wonder
about the old black man slow as summer
with the Mexican child who moves like
a *chapulín*, a grasshopper.

Juan is six now, growing up.
In Georgia, where Pop-pop was raised,
there are cornfields that whish and whisper.
There are fields of corn, too, in Mexico,
where Juan's people come from.
Juan needs to know the song of corn.
Next door there's a vacant lot,
jeweled with bits of broken bottles,
adorned with a car hull
like a huge charred beetle.
"I mean to plant a plot of corn,"
Pop-pop announces, viewing the lot.
"On second thought, *popcorn*."
As that notion spangs into his head,
Pop-pop grins at Juan.

Soon the lot is tall with corn,
the beetle-car overgrown.
Now Juan and Pop-pop know
what it is to turn the soil.
What it is to sweat in the sun.
What it is to pray for rain.
They know what Georgia farmers and Mexican farmers
have always known.
Once, while they work, a boy sneaks
inside the car and pretend-drives, shouting,
"Move over, you son-of-a-turtle!"
Juan loves this noisy driver.
At once they're friends
forever.

Juan loves Chucho because he's wild
as wind. Restless as corn.
But one time, Chucho kneels in the dirt
and cups his hands around a young plant.
"Don't laugh," he says. "I'm going to be a farmer."

That summer Juan turns seven.

From shadowing Pop-pop, at times Juan walks
an old man's walk.
Juan feels all grown up.
So grown up, he wants to help out.
Besides, Pop-pop can't abide
"no gommin' and piddlin' around."
They fix up a stand from crates.
Juan makes the sign himself—NEWBORN CORN,
with a picture of a little cob in a cradle.
He draws it with stubs of crayons, every color
but green. (At age four he ate that one.)
Chucho wants to sell corn too.
Juan has him husk the sweet ears.
Chucho'd rather count the coins they earn,
but that job's for Juan.
After that, in summer, they sit in the sun—
growing up together—in Angel City, selling corn.

A storm comes from nowhere, stinging
the streets with bullet-rain.
Beside the newborn corn, Chucho is struck by a bullet
from a phantom car.
At the hospital, Juan stares at Chucho's window,
its square eyes glassy and blind.
He says, "Please don't die.
When you get well, you can count the money.
I'll husk the corn."
But Chucho dies anyway.
Juan feels numb. At home, he goes outside
and he holds out his arms and turns his face
to the sky. *"Chucho!"*
All his tears fall down. And it rains. And it rains.
Juan is nine.

Every day, when he goes by his door,
Juan nearly knocks, to see if Chucho can play.
Then he remembers. Chucho's not there.
Juan asks, "Pop-pop, will I get to grow up?"
His father gives him a fierce, long hug.
In this city, he wonders, *where's the love?*

Today Juan is ten.
He's so excited, he grasshoppers his way
through the market aisles, looking for a piñata.
He finds the perfect one, a star with streamers
like tassels of corn.
Reminds him of Chucho.
Suddenly sad, Juan lugs it home.

News moves through the building like a cat
thin as a squint.
So now the neighbors are crowded
into Juan's cramped room, rustling
like presents.
To tease him, they sing "*Sapo Verde* to You"
just like the birthday song.
Full of candy, the piñata waits.
Then—Whack! Crack!—
with wild broom-swipes, Juan spills its sweet rain.
"Grab a gob, son!" Pop-pop whoops.
But Juan is gone.

Juan huddles in the old car, looking out
at the corn. He closes his eyes.
And for a moment he sees
Chucho, on his knees, planting seeds.
He hears him tell those seeds,
"Grow, you sons-of-turtles!"
Then Chucho's gone.
Pop-pop's there.
Juan says, "Chucho won't ever be ten."
Juan knows that in his deep heart
he'll always be lonely
for his friend. Pop-pop knows that too.
The old man crawls in and cradles him.
They need no words, just the hymn
of the corn.
A man and a boy in a field green with life.
In Angel City, here is love.

AUTHOR'S NOTE

Angel City was inspired by an article I read in the *Los Angeles Times*. Leon Graves found a Korean baby abandoned in an apartment building near Blood Alley, a rough part of L.A. Graves brought up the child, Roy, as his own, making certain the boy learned the culture of Korea. The two became so close, a headline about them read, "Our blood and skin color may be different, but we're father and son." Because of my experiences with Mexico and the South, I added those elements to the story.   —T.J.

Patricia Lee Gauch, Editor

PHILOMEL BOOKS

A division of Penguin Young Readers Group. Published by The Penguin Group.

Penguin Group (USA) Inc., 375 Hudson Street, New York, NY 10014, U.S.A.

Penguin Group (Canada), 90 Eglinton Avenue East, Suite 700, Toronto, Ontario, Canada M4P 2Y3 (a division of Pearson Penguin Canada Inc.)

Penguin Books Ltd, 80 Strand, London WC2R 0RL, England.

Penguin Ireland, 25 St. Stephen's Green, Dublin 2, Ireland (a division of Penguin Books Ltd.)

Penguin Group (Australia), 250 Camberwell Road, Camberwell, Victoria 3124, Australia (a division of Pearson Australia Group Pty Ltd).

Penguin Books India Pvt Ltd, 11 Community Centre, Panchsheel Park, New Delhi - 110 017, India.

Penguin Group (NZ), Cnr Airborne and Rosedale Roads, Albany, Auckland 1310, New Zealand (a division of Pearson New Zealand Ltd).

Penguin Books (South Africa) (Pty) Ltd, 24 Sturdee Avenue, Rosebank, Johannesburg 2196, South Africa.

Penguin Books Ltd, Registered Offices: 80 Strand, London WC2R 0RL, England.

Text copyright © 2006 by Johnston Family Trust. Illustration copyright © 2006 by Carole Byard.

All rights reserved. This book, or parts thereof, may not be reproduced in any form without permission in writing from the publisher, Philomel Books, a division of Penguin Young Readers Group, 345 Hudson Street, New York, NY 10014. Philomel Books, Reg. U.S. Pat. & Tm. Off. The scanning, uploading and distribution of this book via the Internet or via any other means without the permission of the publisher is illegal and punishable by law. Please purchase only authorized electronic editions, and do not participate in or encourage electronic piracy of copyrighted materials. Your support of the author's rights is appreciated. The publisher does not have any control over and does not assume any responsibility for author or third-party websites or their content.

Published simultaneously in Canada. Manufactured in China by South China Printing Co. Ltd.

Design by Semadar Megged. The illustrations are rendered in acrylic on paper.

Library of Congress Cataloging-in-Publication Data
Johnston, Tony, 1942–   Angel City / Tony Johnston ; [illustrated by] Carole Byard.   p. cm.
Summary: An old black man finds a baby abandoned in a Dumpster and raises him in a rough Los Angeles neighborhood to know both African American and Mexican American ways.
[1. Inner cities—Fiction. 2. Fathers and sons—Fiction. 3. African Americans—Fiction. 4. Mexican Americans—Fiction. 5. Los Angeles (Calif.)—Fiction.] I. Byard, Carole M., ill. II. Title. PZ7.J6478 Amt 2006 [Fic]—dc21   00-040649

ISBN 0-399-23405-5
1 3 5 7 9 10 8 6 4 2
First Impression

TONY JOHNSTON began her career writing stories for her fourth-grade students. Since then, she has published more than one hundred children's books, such as *The Spoon in the Bathroom Wall* and *Any Small Goodness*, displaying her versatility, humor, and warmth to an ever-widening audience.

Mrs. Johnston lives in San Marino, California.

CAROLE BYARD is an award-winning illustrator with a distinguished career in children's books. An exceptional painter and sculptor, she is well-known for her vivid Impressionistic style, and has taught at the Baltimore School for the Arts and Parsons School of Design. Among her many distinctions as an artist are several fellowships and awards from the National Endowment for the Arts, the New York State Council on the Arts, and the Gottlieb Foundation. Her book *Working Cotton* received both the Caldecott and Coretta Scott King Honor in 1993.

Carole Byard lives in Baltimore, Maryland.